for Tim and Emily
with love
~PL

for Aaron
~PI

This edition produced for
The Book People Ltd
Hall Wood Avenue, Haydock, St Helens WA11 9UL, by
LITTLE TIGER PRESS
1 The Coda Centre, 189 Munster Road, London SW6 6AW
First published in Great Britain 2000
Text © 2000 Paeony Lewis
Illustrations © 2000 Penny Ives
Paeony Lewis and Penny Ives have asserted their rights
to be identified as the author and illustrator of this work
under the Copyright, Designs and Patents Act, 1988.
Printed in Belgium by Proost NV, Turnhout
1 3 5 7 9 10 8 6 4 2

I'll Always Love You

by
Paeony Lewis

illustrated by
Penny Ives

TED SMART

One morning Alex woke early
and ran downstairs to the kitchen.
"I'll make Mum some toast and
honey for breakfast," he said.
"She'll like that."

Alex reached for the honey bowl and . . .

CRASH!

His mum's favourite bowl was
now nine pieces of sticky china.

Alex hadn't *meant* to break it. What would she say?

Alex's mum was doing her morning exercises.
"Hello, Alex," she said. "Did I hear something break?"
"Mum, will you only love me if I'm good?" asked Alex.

"I'll always love you," said his mum, and she smiled.

"Even when I've done something that *isn't* good?" asked Alex.

"I'll still love you," said his mum. "Honest."

"What if I have a pillow fight with Joey Bear and
all the feathers burst out? Will you still love me?"
"I'll always love you. Though you must
pick up all the feathers."

"What if I spill my new pots of paint on Baby
Pog and she turns green, red and blue?
Will you still love me?"
"I'll always love you. Though you
will have to bath her."

"What if I forget to close the fridge
door and Baby Pog pulls everything out?
Will you still love me?"
"I'll always love you. Though there
won't be any food for tea."

"What if I pour Grandma Bear's lumpy porridge
all over my head? Will you still love me?"
"I'll always love you. Though you will
have to eat another bowlful.
Now, why are you being
such a silly bear
this morning?"

For a few moments Alex didn't say anything.
Then he whispered, "What if I break your
favourite honey bowl? Will you still love me?"
"You know I'll always love you,"
said his mum. "Come on, Alex,
it must be time for breakfast."

And off they went to the kitchen.

"Oh no!" cried his mum when she saw the pieces of sticky china. "That was my favourite bowl, Alex."

"Sorry," said Alex. Two tears drizzled down his face. "You said you would still love me. I love *you*."

"Of course I love you,"
said his mum, hugging him.

"Hey, I've got an idea!" shouted
Alex, wriggling from her arms.
"What is it?" she asked.
"It's a surprise," Alex said
and he ran off to his bedroom.

He looked in his toybox . . .

He looked in his cupboard . . .

and he looked under his table.

At last Alex found what he wanted.

He got out his new paints, poured
some water into a jam jar and
swirled his paintbrush around.

Alex went to find his mum.
"Look, it's a new bowl," he said. "See, it
says 'Love from Alex'. But be careful, the
paint's still wet."
"I'll be *very* careful," said his mum, smiling.
"Because this is going to be my very
favourite honey bowl!"